For my grandchildren — EA

For those who live sharing their knowledge — MM

Groundwood Books / House of Anansi Press
groundwoodbooks.com

We acknowledge for their financial support of our publishing
program the Canada Council for the Arts, the Ontario Arts
Council and the Government of Canada.

Library and Archives Canada Cataloguing in Publication
Amado, Elisa, author
What are you doing? / Elisa Amado ; Manuel Monroy, illustrator.
— First paperback printing.
Previously published: Toronto: Groundwood Books, 2011.
Issued in print and electronic formats.
ISBN 978-1-77306-004-0 (paperback). —
ISBN 978-1-55498-288-2 (pdf)
I. Monroy, Manuel, illustrator II. Title.
PS8551.M335W43 2017   jC813'.6   C2016-905758-5
C2016-905759-3

The illustrations were done digitally, starting with drawings
in color pencil, and watercolor.
Design by Michael Solomon
Printed and bound in Malaysia

Canada Council   Conseil des Arts
for the Arts   du Canada

ONTARIO ARTS COUNCIL
CONSEIL DES ARTS DE L'ONTARIO
an Ontario government agency
un organisme du gouvernement de l'Ontario

With the participation of the Government of Canada
Avec la participation du gouvernement du Canada | Canadä

MIX
Paper from
responsible sources
FSC® C012700
www.fsc.org

What
Are You
Doing?

Elisa Amado

pictures by
Manuel Monroy

(g) GROUNDWOOD BOOKS   HOUSE OF ANANSI PRESS   TORONTO   BERKELEY

"What are you doing?" called Chepito's
mother as he ran out the door.

"Why, why, why?" sang Chepito.

"School starts today, remember?
We have to go right after lunch.
Don't be late."

"I don't want to go to school," Chepito
sang to himself.

"What are you doing?" asked Chepito.

"Reading the paper," answered the big man.

"Why, why, why?" sang Chepito.

"To see who won the game, of course."

"What are you doing?" asked Chepito.

"I'm reading a comic," answered the girl.

"Why, why, why?" sang Chepito.

"Because Mafalda is so funny."

"What are you doing?" asked Chepito.

"Reading this guidebook," answered
the young woman.

"Why, why, why?" sang Chepito.

"We're lost. Where are we, anyway?"
said the young man.

"What are you doing?" asked Chepito.

"Reading a manual," answered the greasy mechanic.

"Why, why, why?" sang Chepito.

"Because I can't figure out what's wrong with this stupid car."

"What are you doing?" asked Chepito.

"Reading this magazine," answered the young woman.

"Why, why, why?" sang Chepito.

"So I can choose a beautiful new hairdo for the dance tonight."

"What are you doing?" asked Chepito.

"Reading the hieroglyphics on this stela," answered the archeologist.

"Why, why, why?" sang Chepito.

"Because they tell about a war that happened right here more than a thousand years ago when the Maya kings ruled this place."

Chepito got home just in time.

After lunch Chepito's mother and his little sister, Rosita, walked over to the school with him.

Chepito looked into his classroom. He saw a shelf with books on it and decided to go in.

"What are you doing?" he asked the teacher.

"I am going to read this book to you," she
answered.

Chepito ran all the way home from school.
He went in the door and sat down on a
chair. He pulled a book out of his bag.

"What are you doing?" said his mother.

"I'm reading a book," answered Chepito.

"Did you learn how to read on your first day of school?" asked his mother.

"No, but I can tell by the pictures," said Chepito.

"Shall I read you the story, Rosita?" he asked.

"Why, why, why?" she sang.

Chepito was about to say, "Because it's fun."

But before he could, Rosita answered,
"Yes. Read it to me."